# THE MYSTERY AT EAGLE HARBOR

*A Michigan Lighthouse Adventure*

By M.C. Tillson

Illustrated by Lisa T. Bailey

*For Micah who put up with the most,*
*to Lisa as always,*
*to Lloyd and Fran who were there from the start,*
*and to all my friends and encouragers*
*at Eisenhower.*

## THE MYSTERY AT EAGLE HARBOR

Copyright © 2013 by M. C. Tillson
All rights reserved

ISBN 978-0-9764824-1-3
Library of Congress Control Number: 2007902863

**A LIGHTHOUSE ADVENTURE BOOK**
Published by A&M Writing and Publishing
Santa Clara, California
www.amwriting.com

Printed in the U.S.A
First printing, April 2007

# Contents

## Don't Mind Me...

Hi there! Don't mind me. I just thought of a couple of things I'd like you to know before you start reading this book.

In case this is your first Michigan Lighthouse Adventure, you should know that Sam and Becky are in the middle of solving a mystery... well, of *course* you know that—after all, the name of the book pretty much gives it away.

In *The Clue at Copper Harbor*, Sam and Becky visit the lighthouse in the little town of Copper Harbor on Michigan's Upper Peninsula.

There they meet Tom Adams, a ghost who tries to protect the ships and sailors who sail on the Great Lakes. An evil witch named Malina didn't like what Tom was doing, so she put this curse on him:

> Hear my voice, oh magic tower,
> Take this boy's last drop of power,
> Voice and body from him take,
> Drown his magic in the lake,
> Entwine his gifts in riddles three,
> Another's aid the only key.
> From my curse now let him cower,
> Hear my voice, oh magic tower.

The witch's curse took away Tom's ability to help those in trouble, but when Sam and Becky visited the Copper Harbor Lighthouse with their mom and dad, all of that started to change.

You should know that Sam and Becky—the main characters in this book—are not real. This is, after all, a fictional story, and all the characters are made-up people. However, the places I tell you about in this story actually exist on Michigan's magical Upper Peninsula.

## Don't Skip the Hard Words

When you read, do you sometimes skip over words you don't know? Sometimes I do, but most of the time I can figure out what a word means by the other words around it. (That's called **context**.)

**CONTEXT**
(KAHN-tekst)
The words, phrases, or sentences around a word that help explain its meaning

But sometimes the context is not there, or it doesn't give you the exact meaning, so in this book, I've added some definitions for you. If you see a word written in bold letters (like the word *context* above), look around on the same page for a definition of the word. This will help you understand the story better and will also help you add some new words to your vocabulary!

## Check It Out

There are many wonderful books and websites about lighthouses in general and about the lighthouses of the Great Lakes in particular. I've included a list of some of my favorites for you at the end of this book.

# Chapter 1
# ARE WE THERE YET?

"Well, are we?"

"Are we what?" asked Mom as she expertly steered the car around a sharp curve in the road that hugged the northern coast of Michigan's **Keweenaw Peninsula.**

"Are we there yet? Are we?"

"Honestly, honey. You're worse than the kids. We just left Copper Harbor five minutes ago and you're already asking if we're there yet? We're going to Eagle

**KEWEENAW PENINSULA**
(KEY-wah-naw puh-NEN-suh-lah)

The northernmost finger of land that sticks out into Lake Superior from Michigan's Upper Peninsula

9

Harbor—it's only about 15 miles from here—
but first we're going to take a little **detour**
and drive up the Mountain Drive to the top of
Brockway Mountain."

"Yeah, Dad," said Sam, "Aunt Isabel told us
that there are some awesome views along the

**DETOUR**
(DEE-tour)
A different or
roundabout way
of getting to
your destination

way."

"And when you get to the
top," added Becky, "she said
you feel like you can see
forever."

Sam and Becky were spending their summer
vacation on Michigan's Upper Peninsula with
their mom (Alice) and dad (Mike) who were
writing a book about lighthouses.

"So, there's your answer, dear. We're not
there yet, but we will be soon. I suggest you
sit back and enjoy the ride, because once we
get to the top, you're driving and I'm doing the
sightseeing."

The turn-off for the Mountain Drive was
well marked and soon the road started to climb.

Brockway Mountain rises 1,337 feet above sea level (735 feet above lake level), and the road to the top was steep, with many twists and turns.

**HAIRPIN**
(hair-pin)

A sharp U-shaped turn in the road

As they rounded the first **hairpin** curve, Dad shouted, "Alice! Lookout! Lookout! Pull over!"

"Honey! What is it?" Mom quickly pulled the car into the small parking area in front of

them. "Are you OK?"

"I'm fine, but look — there at the sign. It says 'Scenic Lookout' and, as you all know, I'm always lookin' out for a lookout."

Sam, Becky, and Mom groaned as they got out of the car. They had almost gotten used to Dad's love of **puns** and bad jokes... almost.

**PUNS**
(puns)

Jokes made by intentionally using the wrong meaning of a word (or the wrong word)

"Wow!" said Sam as he stood at the edge of the clearing that overlooked the tiny town of Copper Harbor. "You can see everything from here. It's like the postcard I bought at the book store. Look, you can see the house where we stayed and the Harbor Haus restaurant—oh, and there's the dock for the lighthouse tour boats!"

"Look, Mom," said Becky, "there's Aunt Isabel's house and—yikes! Look at the lighthouse with all those rocks around it. You can see why the ships needed some help getting in and out of Copper Harbor."

Mom sighed deeply as she took in the picture-perfect view in front of her. "Can you imagine how this looks in the fall, with the deep blue lake and all the leaves turning orange and red and golden yellow? It must be beautiful…truly spectacular."

"How about in winter," said Dad, "when everything is covered with snow and the edge of the lake is frozen? Can you imagine being a sailor on this lake in the winter? Makes me cold just thinking about it. Brrrrr!" Dad shivered.

"OK, everybody—back in the car before somebody gets frostbite. We have a mountain to climb!"

"Dad, you do realize it's the middle of summer, don't you?" Becky looked at Sam and shook her head as they got back in the car.

"Certainly I know it's summer," Dad replied. "If it wasn't summer, you two would be in school. And you're not, are you? I'm just saying, you can never be too careful."

# Chapter 2
## ON TOP OF THE MOUNTAIN

The Mountain Drive climbed slowly through the woods until all of a sudden it broke free of the forest into an open meadow at the top of Brockway Mountain. And it was true, you *could* see forever—in every direction.

Mom parked the car outside a little gift shop with the fanciful name of Skytop Inn. Before she could even turn off the motor, Dad jumped out of the car and called to Sam and Becky to follow him.

"Look over here, kids!" Dad was pointing north. "Look, there on the horizon! It's clear enough to see all the way to **Isle Royale** today! That's more than 50 miles away.

"Isle Royale is one of our national parks, but it's actually a lot closer to Canada than it is to the United States. There are no roads on it, so no cars. The only way you can get there is by boat or by seaplane. Moose live there—only about 540 of them now—and wolves. People come from all around the world

**ISLE ROYALE**
(Ile ROY-ul)
An 850-square mile island on Lake Superior that was established as a national park on April 3, 1940

to study how they live together on this island and…Ohmygosh! Look over here!"

Before Sam and Becky could finish "ooh-ing" and "ahh-ing" over Isle Royale to the north, Dad pointed them to the west side of the mountain.

"Look over there!" said Dad. "Now you're looking at Eagle Harbor and Agate Harbor. And that little lake right there? That's Lake Bailey... Oh, wow! Look here!"

Grinning, Becky and Sam followed their father's pointing finger and now looked south out over the rest of the Keweenaw Peninsula. "There's Lake Medora, and **Bete Grise Bay** is just beyond that. Didn't I read something about a ship that sank in that bay?"

**BETE GRISE BAY**
(bay-de-GREE bay)

A sheltered inlet of Lake Superior on the south side of the Keweenaw Peninsula ("Bete Grise" means "gray beast" in French)

"That's right," said Sam. "It was on October 23, 1910. The captain tried to find shelter from a huge storm and finally made it to Bete Grise Bay. That night, the ship caught fire and sank. Luckily, all of the crew got off the ship safely."

"All but one," said Becky under her breath. Sam sent her a warning look and shook his head slightly.

Mom looked at Sam quizzically. "How do you know so much about that shipwreck? Is that what you two were doing at the lighthouse in Copper Harbor?"

"That *was* an excellent exhibit," said Dad. "The computer that showed the shipwrecks when you clicked on the map was awesome. But I thought you two were out playing on the rocks and looking for ghosts."

"What!" said Sam and Becky together.

Sam continued, "What do you mean? We weren't looking for ghosts, we were looking for a…ouch!"

Sam jumped as Becky elbowed him in the ribs. "Uh…I mean, why do you say that, Father?"

"I heard what Captain Pete said when he took us over to the lighthouse that first time." He lowered his voice to sound like Captain Pete. "'Aye, keep your eyes open and your mouth closed.'"

"Oh Dad, really," said Becky rolling her eyes.

"Look, kids! Look up! Mike, look!" Mom was looking through her binoculars, but not at the view. Instead, she had them pointed straight up at the sky. "It's an eagle. At least I think it is. Here Mike, you take a look. I thought all the eagles were gone from around here."

"It's an eagle all right. You can tell by looking at his wings. See how they make a nice straight line when he flies? Unfortunately you guys don't get to see too many eagles."

"Look at him," sighed Mom. "Isn't he beautiful? He's just riding the air currents... letting them take him wherever they go. That's the life, isn't it?"

"It's sooo cool!" said Sam. "Watch him—I don't think he's flapped his wings this whole time—he's just gliding."

"Think about the view he has from up there," said Becky, watching the majestic bird circle higher and higher. "He can see the whole Keweenaw Peninsula…maybe even all of Lake Superior. I wish I could fly like that."

They all watched in silence as the eagle continued to circle up and up and up over the mountain until he was no more than a speck in the blue, blue sky.

# Chapter 3
## SKYTOP INN

"Mom, is it OK if Becky and I go over to Skytop Inn?" Sam walked backwards toward the store as he asked.

"Yes, dear. Be careful," Mom answered absently. She was still looking through her binoculars, trying to follow the flight of the lone eagle as long as she could.

Becky and Sam raced each other across the dirt parking lot and up the steps leading to the little gift store. They pulled opened the door and stepped inside.

It was darker inside the store and cooler than out in the hot sun. As their eyes adjusted to the change, Sam and Becky looked around with delight. Skytop Inn was packed full of treasures.

"Oooh…Sam, look at the candy sticks. They must have every flavor in the world."

"Becky, look at all the books! Here's one about the northern lights! And look at these rocks!"

"Sam, look at this moose! Feel how soft he is!"

"Good morning," said a booming voice. "Or is it afternoon already?"

"No," said Sam, "it's still morning—at least for a little while longer."

From behind the counter, a big man with a bushy black beard and sparkling blue eyes stood up and smiled at Sam and Becky.

"Good morning, then. Good morning to the two of you. Is this your first trip to the mountain?"

"Yes it is," said Becky. "We're here with our mom and dad. They're writing a book about lighthouses."

"That so? Well there are lots of 'em around here. Some are even haunted—like the one over in Eagle Harbor."

"That's where we're going next!" said Sam.

"Well, watch your step when you're there. Most of the ghosts I know are pretty friendly, but others…well, you just never know. Now, wait a minute. You two wouldn't happen to be Sam and Becky, would you?"

"Yes, we are. I mean, I am. I mean, I'm Sam and she's Becky. How do you know who we are?"

The man ducked down behind the counter and popped up again, this time with a bright green envelope in his hand.

"Well, my name is Weston and my family owns this store and this mountain. I'm also the postmaster of Copper Harbor, and right before I left to come up the mountain today, a beautiful young lady—all dressed up she was—left this envelope at the post office. She asked if I was coming up the mountain this morning and, if I was, would I mind giving this envelope to Sam and Becky who would be stopping by.

"I told her I would, and I turned around to get a pen to write down her name. But when I turned back, the lady was gone. Strange one that, but very beautiful. Never saw such pretty green eyes...

"Anyway, here you go." Mr. Weston handed the envelope to Becky.

The envelope was about the size of a postcard. On the front, someone had written "Sam and Becky" in fancy handwriting.

"Mr. Weston," said Sam, "Have you ever seen this lady before?"

"No, and I never forget a face. She's not from around here.

"So, you're going over to Eagle Harbor today? Maybe you'll see my friend, Captain Pete. He works up at the Eagle Harbor museums sometimes."

"Oh, we know Captain Pete. He took us over to the Copper Harbor Lighthouse on his boat. Does he still have his laryngitis? He got sick and lost his voice all of a sudden, and we never got to tell him good-bye."

"He's better now," said Mr. Weston. "Seems that it was a very temporary thing. Very strange. One minute he's fine and rambling on about his sailing adventures and the next minute he can't make a sound. I told him *someone* was trying to stop him from talking."

Mr. Weston chuckled and then added, "That'll be the day—when someone stops ol' Pete from talking. Here now, you help yourself to a candy stick and take one to Captain Pete, too. Here's his favorite flavor—butter rum."

"Wow! Thanks, Mr. Weston," said Sam as he chose a watermelon-flavored candy stick.

"Now you be sure and tell Captain Pete that Weston says 'Hello,' OK?"

"We will!" said Becky as she tucked the envelope into the pocket on the back of Sam's backpack and selected a cherry candy stick from the display. "Thanks, Mr. Weston. We like your store."

"And your mountain," added Sam as he opened the door.

"Come again soon." Mr. Weston waved good-bye and dropped back down behind the counter to finish his work.

Sam followed Becky down the steps to find Mom and Dad. Nobody saw the sleek, black cat sitting in the shadows on the front porch, and nobody noticed the cat get up slowly, stretch, and start down the steps after Sam and Becky.

# Chapter 4
# ALL AROUND

"So," said Sam, "do you think we should tell Mom and Dad about the envelope?" He and Becky walked slowly back across the parking lot to their parents.

"I don't know. Maybe we should see what's in it first. Otherwise they'll want to know why some lady is leaving an envelope for us in a place we didn't even know we were going."

"Quick kids, come over here!" Dad stood beside the stone wall at the edge of the parking lot. He was pointing north and looking for all the world like a sea captain on the **bridge** of his ship. "Take a look. There's a sight you don't often see in this day and age.

**BRIDGE**
(brij)
The forward part of a ship where the navigator plots the course for the ship

Down on Lake Superior, Sam and Becky could clearly see three tall sailing ships moving gracefully across the lake toward Eagle Harbor.

"There's going to be a parade of tall ships in Eagle Harbor this coming weekend," said Dad. "The ships are already arriving for the festival. This is terrific! Take a look, kids. This is something you'll probably never see again."

And it *was* a magnificent sight. The tallest ship had over 20 sails—each sail was pulled perfectly **taut**, straining against the wind that was pushing the ship forward.

**TAUT**
(tawt)
Tight, with no wrinkles or slack

With very little effort, you could imagine yourself back in the 1850s, on the deck of one of these tall ships, with the wind blowing your hair. You can almost hear the chatter of the sailors and the loud voice of the **first mate** barking the captain's orders. When you look up, you see the white clouds playing in the brilliant blue sky. Between you and the clouds fly the seagulls pretending to be the sails at the very top of the ship.

**FIRST MATE**
(furst mayt)

The officer on a ship who is in charge after the captain

"Think of the stories that ship could tell if only we had time to listen," sighed Becky.

As the four of them walked back toward the car, she couldn't resist just one more glimpse of the tall ships sailing majestically on beautiful Lake Superior.

*******

"OK, Mike. It's your turn. We need to take Brockway Mountain Drive down the other side of the mountain until we meet up with Highway M-26. That will take us right in to Eagle Harbor."

Mom buckled her seatbelt and adjusted her headrest. "I'm just going to sit back and watch the trees and the flowers and the sky, and then, when we get down the mountain, I'll watch the waves and the shore and the lake."

Dad laughed. "I get it, I get it. I'm driving and you're sightseeing. OK, let's go. All aboard. Anyone want to see anything else? The Statue of Liberty? The Eiffel Tower? The Grand Canyon? A herd of moose…or is it meese? Or mooses? What is the word for many moose?"

They started down the mountain as Dad continued to talk—evidently to himself—about the correct way to refer to a bunch of moose. "Should we look at the envelope now?" whispered Sam to Becky.

"Let's wait until we're by ourselves. Once we know what's in it, we can explain it to Mom and Dad." Becky turned to look out the window.

A few minutes later, Sam leaned over to ask, "Do you think the lady who left the envelope is the witch who put the curse on Tom?"

"Don't you?" whispered Becky in return.

Earlier, in Copper Harbor, Tom had warned Sam and Becky that Malina, the witch who cursed him, could change her appearance to that of any woman—young or old. The only things about her that didn't change were her startling green eyes and the black cat that went with her everywhere.

"I don't know," said Sam under his breath, "but I do think it's pretty weird that we keep crossing paths with all these ladies with green eyes."

Becky bit her lip as she looked out the window. A few minutes later she leaned over to Sam. "If you're right, and it is Malina, why would she leave us an envelope? Come to think about it, why did she help us solve the riddle back at the Copper Harbor Lighthouse?"

"I don't know, Becky. None of it makes any sense. I sure wish Tom was around so we could talk to him about it."

"Me too." Becky turned back to the window.

They were getting near the end of Brockway Mountain Drive. At the bottom of the mountain, Dad turned left onto highway M-26 and headed toward Eagle Harbor.

"You know," said Mom, as she watched the waves lapping hungrily at the big rocks guarding the shoreline, " our rooms won't be ready until after 2:00. We should go ahead and eat, and then we can explore the shoreline a little. I brought some things so we can have a picnic. After we get settled in our rooms, we'll still have some time to visit the lighthouse and explore the town."

"Sounds good," said Dad. "We'll find a place to pull over in the next mile or two. You know, I have to admit I didn't think there was anything special about the Eagle Harbor Lighthouse. I probably would have skipped it and gone on up the peninsula."

"Well, that elderly lady at the Copper Harbor Lighthouse seemed to think it was something not to be missed!" said Mom. "She practically made us promise to go there."

"She did, didn't she? How did she put it, Alice?"

"I remember her exact words," said Mom. "She said, 'There's a great deal to see there if you look at the right place.'"

"*In* the right place, honey," corrected Dad. "*At* the right place doesn't make sense."

"I know. I agree with you, but that's what she said, 'at the right place.'"

"She was a little strange. I wonder where she got that walking stick. I've never seen anything like it. Did you see it, kids? The whole top of the stick was carved like a cat's head. The stick was black—probably made out of **ebony** or something like that. I don't think she really needed it, though. She didn't seem to have much trouble walking."

**EBONY**
EBB-on-nee
A hard, heavy, blackish wood from special trees in southeast Asia

Sam looked at Becky and shrugged his shoulders as he turned back to the window. There sure were a lot of ladies with green eyes around here.

# Chapter 5
## PASTY PROMISES

"Look, Dad!" Becky pointed to a sign by the side of the road. "It says they have Paul Bunyan's footprint. Captain Jack told us Paul Bunyan dug the Great Lakes as a water dish for Babe, his big, blue ox."

"I heard that Paul's footprints made the Great Lakes and Babe's footprints made all the lakes in Minnesota," chimed in Sam. "We read about it in one of the tall tale books in the library."

"Let's check it out," said Dad. "This looks like the perfect place to have lunch."

"I picked up some **pasties** on my walk this morning," said Mom. "Are you hungry?"

"Yes!" chorused Sam and Becky as Dad parked the car near a group of empty picnic tables.

**PASTIES**
(PAST-ees)

A flavorful pastry usually made of ground beef and root vegetables like potatoes, onions, and rutabagas. Best served with ketchup!

Not far from the tables was a mini mountain range of rocks that looked like it would be easy to climb. Sam and Becky could hardly wait to explore.

"We seem to be the only ones here," said Dad. "Looks like we have the run of the place! Where do you want to sit?"

Sam led the way to the table closest to the rocks. The table, sheltered from the wind, was in a garden-like setting with wildflowers growing all around.

"Just what is a pasty?" asked Becky as she helped Dad set the bags of food on the table. Mom was bringing the drinks and some napkins.

"Meat pies," said Mom.

"Oh…boy…" said Sam with a doubtful look on his face, "sounds…uh…ah…yummy?"

"Well, they're really more than just meat pies. They are a treat of the tundra, the Cornish miners' meal, a delicious delight of flaky pastry crust filled with a mouth-watering mixture of…"

"Gee, Mom, are you doing a commercial for these things?" interrupted Sam.

"…a mouth-watering mixture of meat and vegetables," repeated Mom with a pointed look at Sam, "that tempts the taste buds and smiles at your nose...at least that's what the good ones do. The not-so-good ones are very heavy, very solid lumps of meat and potatoes that sit in your stomach like a rock and take weeks to digest.

"But these are good ones," she quickly reassured Sam and Becky as she saw their horrified faces. "These are the really good ones."

Dad had pulled all the pasties and drinks from the bags. He started to unwrap the pasty package nearest to him and then stopped.

"Have you ever noticed that pasties, burritos, and hot dogs have a lot in common?" he asked. Sam exchanged smiles with Becky. Whenever Dad started a conversation with "Have you ever noticed..." you knew it was going to be a very long conversation—probably very interesting, but always very long.

"Think about it," continued Dad, "they all provide people with a way to carry their meals so they can go to work and…"

Sam quietly took two of the pasties from the pile in front of Dad, while Becky selected two cans of cold lemonade. And then, before Mom and Dad noticed, they tiptoed off to the **beckoning** rocks.

**BECKONING**
(BEK-en-ing)
Something that is inviting or attractive

Behind them, they heard Mom joining the conversation: "Well, let's not forget falafels and the whole pita bread thing. And then you have to consider the Earl of Sandwich and all of his contributions to food portability issues…"

Becky and Sam followed the trail as it went up rock steps that were dug into the wall of boulders. At the top they stopped and just stood there in amazement.

The view of Lake Superior was awesome. They were not sheltered from the wind and waves by trees and land as they had been in Copper Harbor. This was the open lake and as far as you could see—all the way to the horizon—there was nothing but the ever-changing waters of Lake Superior.

Today, the wind tossed the clouds in the sky and pushed huge waves across the lake. As the waves collided with the shore and crashed into the rocks, gigantic bursts of water sprayed up like fountains. The spray felt good on this warm summer day.

"The lake definitely has moods, doesn't it?" said Becky. "Yesterday it was so calm and lazy and peaceful, and today…"

"...and today it is *not* in a good mood," said Sam. "In fact, it seems a little angry. I don't want to eat here—everything will be wet before we're finished."

Sam and Becky followed the trail down across the rocks. They found a little hollowed out area behind one of the big rocks that made a bench.

"This is perfect," said Becky. "We even have a table." She pointed at the flat-topped rock right in front of the bench rock.

"This is good," said Sam. "We can see the lake, but it can't see us. At least that's what it feels like."

Sam plopped the pasties down on the flat-topped rock. "Which one do you want?" He unwrapped the packages. "I've got hamburger meat with potatoes and...and hamburger meat with potatoes."

"Hmm, let me see…" said Becky as she opened a can of lemonade. "I think I'll have the hamburger meat with potatoes if you don't mind."

"Good choice," said Sam. "Here you go."

Sam and Becky sat on the bench rock and took their first bites.

"Ummm," said Sam. "Mom was right. These are good."

"I like this place," said Becky, happily munching on her pasty. "It gives me a good feeling. I like being able to see all around, but I like feeling cozy too."

"So, do you think we'll find a riddle in Eagle Harbor?" asked Sam, talking with a mouth full of pasty.

"I don't know, but let's take a look at that envelope. Maybe it will give us some answers.

# Chapter 6
# THE ENVELOPE, PLEASE?

Sam took a gulp of lemonade and then set the can down on the flat rock. He pulled his backpack onto his lap.

"See, this is what I don't understand," he said as he looked in the back pocket. "How in the world are we going to find a riddle? I mean we don't even know for sure that there *is* a riddle in Eagle Harbor, do we?"

He felt around in the back pocket again and then unzipped the front pocket of the backpack while he continued talking. "Tom just said he *thought* it might be there. And even if it is there, where is there? I know Eagle Harbor is pretty small, but where do we even start looking?"

Sam looked puzzled and then stuck his hand in the side pockets of the backpack to feel around. "And what are we looking for? It just seems like we're looking for a needle in the haystack, but we're not even sure there's a needle, or that we're looking in the right haystack. *Where* is that envelope?"

By now Sam had looked in every single pocket in his backpack. He had zipped and unzipped everything at least twice, but still he found no envelope.

"I put it in the back pocket of your backpack when we were getting our candy in the store," said Becky. "Are you sure it's not there?"

"Here, you look," said Sam handing the backpack to Becky. She looked again in all the pockets, and even in the secret compartment in the bottom, but there was no envelope to be found.

"We need that envelope," said Sam. "What if it had the clue to the riddle?"

"We need that envelope."

"I just said that, Becky. I agree with you, but you don't have to keep saying it."

"Uh...Sam...I didn't say anything," said Becky quietly.

"Hi Becky! Hi Sam!" said a familiar voice.

"Hi Tom...it is you, isn't it Tom?"

"Yup, it's me. Those pasties look good. They used to be one of my favorite things to eat before...well, you know...before I died and became a ghost. So how are you? What are you doing here? And where's this envelope you keep talking about?"

"Hold on a minute Tom," laughed Becky. "One question at a time. We're fine. We're on our way to Eagle Harbor to see the lighthouse. We're staying at the Harbor View Inn. They say it's haunted—hey, do you know anything about that?"

"That's where *I'm* staying!" said Tom. "I guess that means it *is* haunted—although I haven't seen any other ghosts since I've been there. I *did* see some strange things in the fishing museum where the lighthouse keeper's assistant used to live, but that doesn't mean…"

"Tom," Sam interrupted, "we think the witch gave us an envelope with a clue to the next riddle."

Sam's words tumbled over each other as he told Tom how a lady with green eyes had left an envelope to be delivered to Sam and Becky at Skytop Inn. And how the postmaster, Mr. Weston, gave them the envelope. And how, even though Becky put the envelope safely in Sam's backpack, they couldn't find it now.

"Do you think you left it in the store on the mountain?" asked Tom.

"No," said Sam, "I'm sure we didn't. I saw it when I put my backpack down beside Mom. Don't you remember, Becky? We were looking at the tall ships with Dad, and that black cat was playing with the little squeezy baseball I have on the zipper pull on my backpack, and…"

Sam stopped talking and his eyes got huge. "Becky, you don't think…"

Becky clapped her hands over her mouth. "The cat! Maybe the witch's cat took the letter from your backpack!"

"No way," said Sam, "No way. I don't believe it. Cats can do a lot of things, but they can't take an envelope out of the pocket of a backpack. Cats can't do that…can they?"

"Cats that belong to witches can," said Tom.

In the silence that followed Tom's statement, the crashing of the waves against the rocks got louder and louder. The lake agreed with Tom.

"So why did she give it to us?" Sam blurted out. "I mean, why would she go to all the trouble to give us the envelope just to have her cat take it away?"

"I know," said Tom, "I don't understand either. Why would Malina help me solve the riddle at all? It just doesn't make sense."

"It's almost as if there were two witches," said Becky, thinking out loud. "One is a good witch who tries to help us solve the riddles and the other is an evil, mean witch who's trying to stop us."

"Sam! Becky! Where are you?" At the sound of Dad's voice, Sam scrambled up to the rock tops and waved to his father, who was carefully picking his way across the rocks.

"C'mon kids. It's time to go. I think I just found Paul Bunyan's footprint. A big footprint full of water right here in the cement. And I just stepped in it—right up to my ankle."

"That must be it, Dad!" Sam laughed. "Congratulations for putting your best foot forward—or in your case, putting your best foot right in it."

"Thank you, Samuel. I'll try to remember to laugh at your little joke when I get some dry socks on my feet." Dad sat down on a rock and took off his wet shoe. He pulled off his sock, wrung it out, and put it back on.

"Where were you guys anyway? And who were you talking to? I thought I heard somebody else talking. Was it Paul Bunyan? If so, I have a couple of things I'd like to say to him myself."

Dad pulled his shoe back on. "OK, let's go. Mom's waiting. She wants to check in at the inn so we can visit the lighthouse before it closes."

Dad started back down the path ahead of Becky and Sam. Step-squish, step-squish, step-squish. "I can see you smiling, Sam," he called back. "You better be careful — Mr. Bunyan may have left more than one footprint around here."

"Yeah, Sam," said Becky, "this is one time you *don't* want to follow in Dad's footsteps."

# Chapter 7
## AT EAGLE HARBOR

It was after 2:00 in the afternoon, when Sam, Becky, Mom, and Dad checked into the Harbor View Inn. Their rooms were perfect and had a fantastic view of the harbor and the lighthouse.

"Can we go see the lighthouse now? I want to know if it's really haunted," said Becky.

"Yeah, 'time's a'wastin',' as they say," said Sam. "I want to see the lighthouse, but I also want to see the museums—especially the fishing museum. I heard it had a lot of really interesting exhibits."

"Actually...I'm thinking about a nap," said Dad with a yawn and a slow stretch. "But... if everybody's ready to go, then let's go!" He jumped up from the overstuffed chair where he'd been lounging, and headed for the door. "I'll just take a nap before I go to bed tonight," he called over his shoulder.

Sam and Becky laughed as they followed Dad out the door. They crossed the street and walked the short distance along the path to the Eagle Harbor Lighthouse.

The lighthouse is part of a group of buildings sitting on the west side of Eagle Harbor that's known as the Eagle Harbor Lightstation Complex. The building at the entrance to the lighthouse used to be a garage, but now has exhibits about copper and local mining operations.

The two-story white building (known as the "white house") was originally on the other side of the harbor. It was part of the famous Eagle Harbor Life Saving Station whose brave men saved many lives on Lake Superior. It was moved across the harbor in 1932 and became the assistant lighthouse keeper's house. Today it houses a commercial fishing museum.

The Eagle Harbor Lighthouse was built in 1851 after copper had been found in local mines. The town of Eagle Harbor had no useable roads—especially in winter—so everything coming into Eagle Harbor (food, supplies, building materials, and people) came in on a ship.

Like the lighthouse in Copper Harbor, the Eagle Harbor Lighthouse was first built out of cheap materials that didn't stand up very well to the winds and storms of Lake Superior. Twenty years later, the original lighthouse was torn down and a sturdy red brick building was built in its place.

On the other side of the lighthouse stands the old fog signal building. On days when the fog hid the lighthouse beacon, the foghorn warned approaching ships about the rocky dangers. The fog signal building is now a **maritime** museum.

**MARITIME**
(MARE-i-time)
Having to do with the sea or sailors

And, in the grassy area in front of the buildings, sits a black, two-door, 1927 Chrysler Model 60.

"OK," said Sam, "why is there an old car parked in the middle of the lighthouse courtyard? Don't they have a parking lot? Isn't that guy going to get a ticket for parking there?"

Mom laughed. "Come on, let's go inside. I'm sure we'll find out more."

"Good afternoon!" said the smiling woman behind the desk. "Welcome to the Eagle Harbor Lightstation Complex. Are you visiting from out of town?"

"Yes we are," said Dad. "We're from way out of town."

"It's a pretty safe guess isn't it?" confided the receptionist. "I know everybody in town and most everybody on the peninsula, so I also know all the strangers in town. Where are you from?"

"We're from Northern California," said Sam. "My mom and dad are writing a book about Michigan lighthouses. We were just in Copper Harbor and now we're here to see *your* lighthouse!"

"How exciting! From California *and* writing a book! You know, this is your lucky day. Mrs. Everington, the president of the Upper Peninsula Society for the Preservation of Historical Treasures of the Great State of Michigan is giving her lecture presentation today. She knows more about Eagle Harbor than anyone else I know. She's just about ready to start, so go ahead and take your seats."

Sam and Becky took seats by the door. If Mrs. Everington was anything like Ranger Leslie at the Copper Harbor Lighthouse, they planned to make a quick getaway. Mom and Dad, on the other hand, made a **beeline** for two empty seats in the front row.

**BEELINE**
(BEE-line)
A straight, direct route.

A few minutes later, Sam and Becky realized with delight that Mrs. Everington was not like Ranger Leslie—she was a *storyteller*.

# Chapter 8
# THE STORYTELLER

"Have you ever been on the deck of a ship you knew was going to sink?" asked Mrs. Everington as she walked to the front of the room.

"Close your eyes.

"Now picture yourself on the deck of a huge ship made entirely of steel. It's 444 feet long—that's longer than four football fields put end-to-end—and it weighs over 3,690 *tons*. This ship is a steamer, which means it uses steam to turn the two huge propellers that move it. Night and day, the crew shovels coal into the furnace to feed the hungry fire to make steam.

**WHOLE GALE FORCE**
(hol gail fors)

In the Beaufort measuring system, wind that's blowing from 55-72 miles per hour; a hurricane force wind blows at more than 73 miles per hour

"It's the last day of November in 1926. Ice has formed around the edge of Lake Superior. Under your feet, the deck is a sheet of ice—it's almost impossible to stand up. Snow and sleet are blowing all around. Your beard is frozen solid and your eyelashes keep freezing your eyes shut. The wind is already blowing at **whole gale force**. It is, in fact, a dark and stormy night.

"That's how one sailor felt as he stood on the icy deck of the ship called the *City of Bangor*.

"The ship is upbound, traveling from Detroit, Michigan to Duluth, Minnesota and it's already overdue because of the fierce storms moving onto Lake Superior. You're supposed to be up on the bow—the front of the ship—so you can be lookout.

"Your cargo is—of all things—a load of brand new automobiles. There are over 230 new Chryslers down below in the hold, and more on deck—making it even more difficult to see and get around on this treacherous night.

"All of a sudden, the wind picks up with an angry howl. The captain steers the ship as close to the coastline as he dares, hoping to find some protection from the force of the storm. The problem is that the ice is thicker here. Any minute the angry wind and waves could throw the ship onto the frozen shore or even crash it into another ship!

"There's a slight break in the rain, but the wind has actually gotten stronger—sometimes gusting up to more than 75 miles a hour—that's a *hurricane* force wind! All you can see are dark gray waves on an even darker lake and dark gray clouds churning across the sky.

"The waves are crashing over the side and tossing the huge ship around like a toy boat. Eighteen cars that were on deck have already been washed overboard. You've got a rope tied around your waist to keep from being washed overboard, but now you're thinking one rope may not be enough.

"The wind howls like a hungry wolf. The waves are relentless—crashing over and over against the front and the side of the ship drenching the deck. Suddenly, a giant wave—a rogue wave, bigger than all the others—comes over the side. If the rope doesn't hold, you're gone for sure!"

Mrs. Everington paused and took a sip of water. Becky, Sam, and the rest of the audience held their breath.

"The wave didn't take you, but it drowned the fire in the engine room—the fire that makes the steam that powers the ship. Without the fire, there's no more steam…which means no more power…which means you're at the mercy of the storm and the lake.

"You hear screams. You turn and see one of your mates slip over the edge. Luckily, he also has a rope tied around his middle.

"'Man overboard!' you yell. Everyone grabs at the rope and pulls. The frozen rope cuts through your gloves, but still everyone keeps pulling. The load is heavy—that's good. It means the sailor is still tied on.

"Finally, with everyone working together, you pull the sailor from the lake's deadly grip. "Now the captain shouts to the first mate 'go hard to **port**' and above the screams of the wind, another, more horrific sound tears through the night.

**PORT**
(port)

The left side of a ship (The right side is "starboard")

"The wind and waves have driven the *City of Bangor* directly into the huge boulders near shore—the boulders that kill ships. The wounded ship gives a great shudder as its **hull** rips open. Another giant wave crashes over the bow, tossing the ship and its crew into the shallow waters.

**HULL**
(hull)

The frame or body of a ship

"Without her fire, the *City of Bangor* is doomed. Soon the ship's lifeless smokestack is encased in ice. Icicles hang from every line. Eventually, water freezes over the entire ship, turning it into a huge iceberg. The ship known as the *City of Bangor* is dead.

"The sailors abandon ship. They swim to shore and stagger out of the water onto the cold, rocky shore. You help pull the men who can't swim out of the water before the lake can take them. For now, everyone is safe on shore—but for how long?

"Everyone huddles together to keep from freezing. Is it possible the storm is getting worse?

"And then, just when it seems that everyone is doomed to die in the cold fury of the storm, the winds pause for a breath. The frozen rain and snow continue, but not as hard as before. The storm, at last, is passing.

"By dawn, the wind, frozen rain, and snow have calmed down enough for everyone to move above the beach and onto more solid ground. Some crew members are so exhausted that they beg you to let them lie down and die.

"The cold is intense and everyone has frostbite...or worse. The rocky shore is a quieter, calmer prison than the ship, but it's still a prison. And to make things even worse, you can see storm clouds gathering on the northern horizon for another attack.

"And then...is it a trick? One of the sailors stood up and cupped his ear. Voices! And they're coming from the lake.

"'We'll be back,' the voices call out over the water. 'Take heart...we *will* return!'

"The brave men of the Eagle Harbor Lifesaving Station had already saved 22 men aboard the *Thomas Maytham*, another ship destroyed by the storm that night.

"After delivering that first crew safely to Copper Harbor, the heroes returned to rescue the exhausted sailors from the *City of Bangor*.

"And even though the ship was a total loss, the captain, and all 29 crew members survived. And, when it got cold enough for the water around the steamer to freeze solid, local townspeople helped drive the almost 230 Chryslers—still in good condition—over the ice to Copper Harbor."

When Mrs. Everington finished her story, there wasn't a sound in the room.

And then, as if on **cue**, everyone started breathing again.

**CUE**
(qyu)
A signal to begin a specific action or speech

"Wow."

Slowly the ferocious waves of Lake Superior that Mrs. Everington had conjured in their imaginations gave way to the gentle lapping of waves against the Eagle Harbor shore.

At the front of the room, a man stood up and started clapping.

Soon everyone in the hall was standing and applauding, offering Mrs. Everington the honor of a standing ovation for her amazing storytelling talent.

"Thank you, everyone. Thank you. I'm glad you enjoyed my story. And now, if anybody has any questions, I'd be happy to answer them."

Hands jumped up all over the room.

Mrs. Everington laughed. "I see there's a lot of curiosity here." She pointed at Mom. "Let's start with you."

Without even looking at each other, Sam and Becky slipped out the door. Once Mom and Dad got started with their questions, it would be a while before they were ready to go.

And Sam and Becky had a riddle to find in Eagle Harbor.

# Chapter 9
# A WORD IN EDGEWISE

In the open area between the mining museum and the white house, Becky and Sam stopped to look around.

"*Now* I understand why there's a car parked here," said Sam. "That's one of the cars they saved from the shipwreck, isn't it? Wasn't that story awesome?"

"She is a great storyteller," agreed Becky, walking around the car. She smiled at a little girl with long black braids sitting on the fence on the other side of the car.

"Couldn't you just feel the sleet slamming against your face? I would love to be able to tell a story like that."

"Hi," called the little girl, waving to Sam and Becky. She was swinging her legs and eating a chocolate ice cream cone — at least that was Becky's best guess. She couldn't be certain because there wasn't a lot of ice cream left in the cone. Most of it was on the little girl: on her shirt, on her hands, and all *over* her face — even under the purple sunglasses she wore.

Sam and Becky waved back and then Becky said, "OK, what are we going to do now? Where is Tom? How are we going to find the riddle? And…Sam, are you listening to me?"

Sam wasn't listening. He was watching the little girl finish her ice cream cone. She systematically licked the ice cream off the sides and then nibbled the cone all the way around without stopping. She licked the ice cream in the middle three times and then she started the process all over again.

She nibbled and licked until the ice cream and the cone were completely gone…at least the cone was gone.

Becky smiled at the little girl. "Do you have a napkin?"

"The ice cream's all gone. I don't need a napkin."

"Oh yes you do," said Sam. "You can't see your face, but we can. And you *do* need a napkin."

Becky handed the little girl a crumpled but clean napkin left over from lunch. "Here, use this."

The little girl took the napkin and wiped her mouth. Some of the ice cream came off, but most of it stayed on, giving her a chocolate **mustache**.

**MUSTACHE**
(MUSS-stash)
Hair growing on a person's upper lip

"Thanks," she said. "My name is Reenie. What's your name?"

But before either Sam or Becky could reply, Reenie took a big breath and continued.

"Reenie is a nickname. Do you have a nickname? I'm six years old. One, two, three, four, five, six. How old are you? I have a cat on my shirt. It's made out of black **sequins**. Do you like cats? I'm from Michigan. I'm from the thumb part of the mitten. Do you know about the mitten? I learned about the mitten in kindergarten. It's how we know where we live. Where do you live?"

**SEQUINS**
(SEE-quins)

Tiny, flat shiny plates used to decorate clothing and other items

"Well," said Becky, trying to get a word in edgewise, "we live in California, near..."

"I have an uncle in California. He lives near the ocean...the Pacific Ocean because that's the ocean near California. Have you ever seen the Pacific Ocean?"

"Actually," started Sam, "we..."

"I saw the ocean once, only it was the Atlantic Ocean, not the Pacific Ocean. Have you ever seen the Atlantic Ocean? I've never seen the Pacific Ocean."

Becky and Sam said nothing. They just waited a second, and sure enough, Reenie continued.

"Are you visiting Eagle Harbor? I like Eagle Harbor. Did you see the fish museum in the white house? I like the fish museum. Have you seen the lighthouse? I like the lighthouse. Did you know it was haunted? Do you believe in ghosts? Captain Pete said the ghost walked last night because he couldn't sleep. The ghost, not Captain Pete. Captain Pete sleeps a lot. And he snores when he sleeps. Do you snore?"

"Wait a minute," said Sam holding both hands up to stop the stream of Reenie's conversation. "Do you know Captain Pete?"

"Sure! Everybody knows Captain Pete. He's in the fish museum today," said Reenie, pointing to the two-story white house beside the lighthouse. "I just saw him in there."

"Are you here by yourself, Reenie?" asked Becky, looking around for a family that would belong to this talkative six-year old.

"I have to go now," said Reenie jumping off the fence. "Thanks for the napkin." She held out the chocolate mess to Becky who wrinkled her nose, but took the sticky napkin between her thumb and forefinger.

Becky turned around to put the napkin in the trashcan a few yards away. She called back to Reenie, "Don't you think you should wait for your mom and dad or whoever you're with?"

Becky tossed the napkin in the trash and turned back to Sam and Reenie, but only Sam was there, reading his brochure about all the buildings in the Eagle Harbor Lightstation complex.

"Sam, where is she?"

"She's right here…" Sam looked back at the fence, turned back to the car, and then back to the fence. "Where is she?"

"I don't know. I thought she was here with you. Did you see her run off?"

"No, I didn't. Didn't she go with you?"

Becky shook her head, "No, I just turned around to throw away the napkin. Are you sure you didn't see which way she went?"

"Nope. It's like she just disappeared."

"Well I guess she knows where she's going. She sure can talk a lot, can't she?" Becky looked around one more time for the little girl.

"Did you hear what she said Captain Pete said about the ghosts walking last night?"

"Do you think Tom was one of the ghosts?"

"I don't know," said Sam as he shoved the brochure in his pocket, "but I think we should find Captain Pete."

Keweenaw County
Historical Society's
Eagle Harbor
Lightstation Complex
(Whew!)

# Chapter 10
## GONE FISHING

Sam stopped at the door to the white house. "Do you have any money?" he asked Becky. "Do you know how much it costs to get into the museum?"

"Let's just go to the information desk and ask for Captain Pete. We don't have to pay to do that."

Sam pushed opened the door, but before they could even step inside, a cheery voice called out, "Welcome, welcome, welcome! Welcome to the Keweenaw County Historical Society's

Eagle Harbor Lightstation Complex. This is our Commercial Fishing Museum, a fabulous foray into fishing facts and fiction.

"Come in, come in! You're visitors aren't you? Well, of course you are. You're visiting the museum aren't you for goodness sakes? I'm Miss Maple and I'm the official greeter for today, so welcome, welcome, welcome!"

Miss Maple was a very thin, very smiley, very fluttery woman. She wore a floaty dress that hovered around her when she moved.

"Thank you," said Becky. "We *are* visiting— our parents are back at the history museum talking to Mrs. Everington. We just heard her awesome story about the *City of Bangor* and…"

"Oh my," said Miss Maple, clasping her hands dramatically. "Didn't you just *shiver* with that icy rain smacking you in the face and couldn't you just *feel* the wind trying to blow you overboard?

"I've heard that story hundreds of times and I never get tired of it. I'm glad everyone made it safely to shore, though. I don't think I could listen to it so many times if it didn't have a happy ending. But I'm talking too much. Let's get you signed in and then I can show you around."

Miss Maple pointed to the guest book on the desk and gave Becky a pen. As Becky signed the register, Miss Maple read over her shoulder.

"Sam...and...Becky...Wait, are you Sam and Becky from California?"

"Yes ma'am, we are," said Sam. "How did you know that?"

"I have something that belongs to you," said Miss Maple. She opened the top desk drawer and pulled out a bright green envelope with "Sam and Becky" written on the front. It was the same envelope Mr. Weston had given to them at Skytop Inn.

"A young lady came by just a little while ago. She asked if she could leave this for Sam and Becky from California who would be visiting later today. Lovely woman. She had the most exotic green eyes."

Becky and Sam were so surprised they could hardly speak. Sam took the envelope, while Becky murmured, "Thank you."

"You're very welcome, dears."

Miss Maple floated back to the front of the desk. "So, did you come in for anything in particular today? The lake trout exhibit? The 'Lure of the Loon' room?"

"We were looking for Captain Pete," Sam said. "We heard he was here and we'd like to speak to him if we could."

Miss Maple's bottom lip came out just a bit and her dress stopped fluttering. She put her hands on her hips and turned her back on Sam and Becky.

"Everyone comes to see Captain Pete," she sniffed.

"I'm sorry," Becky started, "we…"

But just at that moment, the front door opened and a family of five walked into the museum.

Miss Maple smiled brightly again. "I guess I should get back to my duties. I see other guests arriving." She fluttered and floated back to the front of the museum, and then called to them over her shoulder, "Captain Pete is upstairs."

As they walked toward the steps, Becky and Sam heard Miss Maple greeting the new visitors. "Welcome, welcome, welcome! Welcome to the Keweenaw County Historical Society's Eagle Harbor Lightstation…"

# Chapter 11
# AT THE TOP OF THE STAIRS

"They'll be here, laddie. I'm sure of it. Don't get your knickers in a knot. You can count on Sam and Becky."

Becky and Sam heard low voices inside the room at the top of the stairs. They walked in and saw Captain Pete sitting in a rocking chair in front of the fireplace, whittling a piece of driftwood, and talking to himself—or so it seemed.

Exhibits about the local fishing industry filled the room. On the mantel above the fireplace perched a beautiful, life-size carving of a rainbow trout, and above the trout hung a huge mirror in the shape of a cloud.

"Captain Pete!" called Sam joyfully. "You're here. We found you!"

"Was I lost, son? Been here the whole time — except, of·course, when I wasn't."

"Sam! Becky! I thought you'd never get here!"

"Tom, is that you?" smiled Becky. "We had no idea how to find you, so we thought we should find Captain Pete and see if he knew where you were."

"So we did," said Sam, "and he does, and you're here!"

"And I'm glad *you're* here," said Tom, "but I've got some bad news. We're running out of time — or at least I am."

"What are you talking about, Tom?"

"I was just about to explain it to Captain Pete," said Tom with a deep sigh. "Last night I met the ghost who lives in the Eagle Harbor Lighthouse. He told me he heard Malina bragging that I would never solve the riddles in time. It turns out that once the first riddle is solved, I only have until the next full moon to solve the other riddles. If I don't solve all three riddles by then, the curse becomes permanent—it can never be reversed."

"I didn't know that," said Becky. "Did you, Tom?"

"Nope. It seems to be a small detail Malina forgot to tell me when she put the curse on me."

"So when's the next full moon?" asked Sam.

"Three days away," said Captain Pete, rocking slowly in his chair and rubbing his beard. "That's why young Tom is so upset. He's only got a few days to figure out two more riddles."

"And I don't even know where the riddles are!" exploded Tom.

"Sam, show him the envelope!" said Becky.

"What envelope?" asked Tom. "I thought the cat took the envelope."

"Maybe it did," said Sam, "but someone — or some*thing* — got it back for us. Here it is!" He held up the green envelope for everyone to see.

"You see, when we got here to the fish museum, Miss Maple asked us to sign the guest register. Then, when Becky wrote our names…"

"Sam," said Tom, "give us the details later, but right now, OPEN THE ENVELOPE!"

"Here, Becky, you open it. I'm too nervous."

Sam handed Becky the envelope. She carefully tore open the flap and looked inside.

No letter. No card. But inside, in the bottom corner of the envelope, Becky saw a small, folded piece of paper.

Sam peeked over Becky's shoulder to look in the envelope. "What's in there? Is it the riddle?"

"I don't know. I don't see anything except this little piece of wadded up paper," said Becky. She handed the ball of paper to Sam to unfold. "So what does it say, Sam?"

"Go ahead, Sam, read it," said Tom.

"Well, there's a little poem, but I can't read the rest. I've never seen anything like this before."

"Stop fooling around, Sam," said Becky. "You've been reading since you were two years old. Just read what's on the paper."

"OK, the poem says:

> Solve the riddle,
> Don't dare miss,
> When in doubt,
> Reflect on this.

"Now read the rest," said Tom.

"I can't—it's like it's in a different language. Here, Becky, you try it."

Becky looked at the writing on the paper and made a face. "I can't read it either. This is weird."

"Now wait right there, young lady," said Captain Pete. "What do you mean you can't read it? Are you telling me none of you youngins' can read what's on a simple piece of paper?"

"Here, Captain Pete," said Becky "you take a look for yourself. It's a kind of code or something."

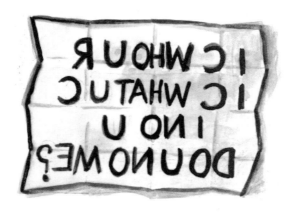

"Well I'll be…" said the Captain. "… this doesn't say anything. It's just a bunch of backwards or upside down letters…or something. What do you think, Tom?"

"I don't know what to think. I mean, it's great we found the riddle, but if we can't even read it, how are we going to solve it? I don't understand." Tom's words were full of disappointment.

For a while no one spoke.

"I can't stand it," said Tom. His voice kept getting louder and then softer like he was pacing up and down the room.

"I'll never get rid of this stupid curse. Do you know there was a scuba diver over at Bete Grise Bay who almost died yesterday? He was exploring the shipwreck of the *Langham*, and got his foot caught in a hole on the deck. I didn't know about the trouble he was in because I didn't have my powers. And then, when I did find out, I couldn't do anything except watch because nobody can see me. He almost ran out of air before his friend helped him get untangled. I hate this curse."

"Don't worry, Tom," said Becky. "We'll help you solve this. I know we can do it. Sam's the second best person I know at figuring out codes."

"Who's the best person?" asked Tom.

"I am," smiled Becky. And while Sam rolled his eyes, Becky held out her hand to Captain Pete for the little piece of paper.

"It's familiar, but it's not," sighed the Captain as he handed the paper to Becky.

"It's like I can almost read it, but I can't," said Tom.

Voices came up from the downstairs hall and then footsteps sounded on the stairs. Someone was coming.

"Shhh," said Captain Pete softly. "Keep your eyes open and your mouth closed."

The next minute, Dad popped his head into the room. "Here you are! We've been looking all over for you two. Didn't you hear your mother and me calling you?" Dad walked into the room with a frown on his face.

"Sorry, Dad," said Becky. "We were just talking to Captain Pete."

"Good afternoon, Captain," said Dad. "I hope you've gotten over your bout of laryngitis."

"That I have, that I have. Thank you for asking. And where is that lovely wife of yours?"

"Right now she's probably standing in front of the lighthouse with steam coming out of her ears. She wants to go inside, but I asked her to wait for the kids and me. If I make her wait much longer, she'll have that ghost after me."

"What ghost are you talking about, Dad?" asked Sam.

"Mrs. Everington told us there's a ghost living in the lighthouse. I'll bet your mother's talking to it right now and asking him to come and find us. Come on, kids. I don't want to be haunted for the rest of my life. Take care, Captain." Dad turned and started down the stairs.

"By the way, Captain Pete," said Sam, "Mr. Weston sent this. He said butter rum was your favorite." Sam handed Captain Pete the candy.

"He's right. It is my favorite. Old Weston knows me too well. Thank you, son. You take care now, and don't forget to reflect on the things you learned today." Captain Pete winked at Sam. "I'll be here early tomorrow if you want to come by."

"Thanks Captain. We'll see you later," said Becky as she walked toward the door. Then she turned back to whisper, "See you tomorrow too, Tom."

"I hope so, Becky," said Tom softly. "I hope so."

# Chapter 12
## DOUBLE TAKE

Sam and Becky sat on the fence outside the Eagle Harbor Lighthouse waiting for Mom and Dad. The four of them had spent the last hour looking at the amazing exhibits inside.

The rooms in the lighthouse were set up the way they might have been when the lighthouse was rebuilt in 1871. There were even **mannequins** dressed like the first lighthouse keeper and his family might have dressed, so visitors could see how it would be to live in the lighthouse back then.

**MANNEQUIN**
(MAN-e-ken)
A life-size figure used to represent a person

"Did you know that the Coast Guard guy who stayed in the lighthouse in 1976 asked to be transferred somewhere else because ghosts kept waking him up?" Sam was reading his brochure again. "And did you notice the lighthouse tower is red on one side and white on the other? That's because the red paint faded so much that the sailors complained they

couldn't see the lighthouse during the day. So they repainted the part that you see from the water a bright white."

Becky walked toward the lake so she could see the side of the octagonal tower. "Oh, yeah, I see what you mean. That's pretty weird. I can see where the two colors meet. I wish we could go up to the top."

"I guess since it's still a real lighthouse they only want the Coast Guard people who check the light to go up there."

"You're probably right. Hey, do you think the ghost in the lighthouse is home? Maybe he could help us figure out what that paper says. It's so frustrating," said Becky.

"I know," agreed Sam, looking up from the brochure. "It's not a normal code. You know, substituting letters for other letters. It's more like a different language, except somehow the letters look familiar. And that doesn't make sense unless I know another language that I forgot I knew."

"What?" said Becky. "That doesn't make any sense. If you know another language, then…"

"Who are you?" interrupted a childish voice behind them. They turned around to see a little girl with long black braids and a sequined cat shirt.

"My name is Becky and this is my brother Sam. We talked to you a little while ago, remember? When you were eating your ice cream cone? Your name is Reenie, right?"

"No, my name is Leena. It's a nickname and I don't remember you at all. I think you're telling me a lie."

"Then why did you tell us your name was Reenie when we saw you before?"

"I didn't."

"Are you saying you didn't tell us your name was Reenie?"

"I didn't see you before."

"Weren't you sitting on the fence over there eating chocolate ice cream in a sugar cone and talking to us about the Pacific Ocean and the Atlantic Ocean?" asked Sam.

"There are no oceans near here," cut in Leena. "These are lakes. The closest ocean is…"

"I KNOW where the closest ocean is," said Sam. "That's not the point. Why did you say your name was Reenie if it really is Leena?"

"I didn't tell you my name was Reenie, because my name is Leena and I don't remember about the oceans because I never talked to you before. Maybe you were talking to someone else. Maybe you were talking to my twin sister."

"You have a twin sister? Well, that would explain it, don't you think? You might have told us you have a twin sister at the beginning," grumbled Sam. "What's your sister's name?"

"Reenie."

"Aaugh! Why didn't you say that before?"

"You didn't ask me. I never tell anybody anything unless they ask and sometimes I don't even tell them when they do ask. I don't like people much," said Leena.

Sam and Becky exchanged glances. Talking to this little girl was like getting caught in sticky tape.

"It seems to me," said Sam slowly, "chances are very good that the little girl we talked to who looked just like you and said her name was Reenie is your twin sister, don't you think?"

"Well, DUH! Of course she is." Leena stuck her tongue out at Sam.

"I have to say that your sister was a lot nicer to talk to than you are…even if she did talk a lot."

"Reenie always talks too much to everybody. She's such a goody-goody. I don't like her—besides I'm mad at her now because she took my sunglasses."

"You have very pretty eyes, Leena," said Becky quietly. "Look at her eyes, Sam. Aren't they a pretty shade of green?"

"Leena," said Sam, "does your sister have green eyes too?"

"Of course. We're twins, remember? We look exactly alike."

"Where is Reenie now?" asked Becky casually.

"I don't know and I don't care," said Leena. "Maybe she's talking to that mean old Captain Pete." She jumped down from the fence "I have to go wash up for dinner."

"Kids! Let's go!" Becky and Sam turned to see Mom and Dad coming out of the lighthouse and waving at them. "Come on, we're going back to the inn for dinner."

"OK!" Sam and Becky waved and turned back to say good-bye to Leena. But there was no one there.

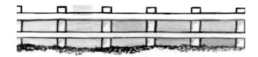

"Wow," said Becky as they started back to the inn behind Mom and Dad. "I guess that explains that. There are two of them, and even though they look exactly alike, they couldn't be more different."

"I know," said Sam. "Reenie was nice even if she did talk a lot. Leena on the other hand… why is she so mean? And what do you think about those green eyes?"

"You think Leena is the witch, don't you?" said Becky under her breath.

"Yes, I do!" said Sam. "She has the green eyes, she has the nickname "Leena"—which is probably short for Malina—and she's mean. Tom said Malina could disguise herself to be a woman of any age—and that includes a six-year old girl.""

"If Leena is a witch, does that mean Reenie is a witch? A witch who looks like Malina— whatever she looks like at the time—but a nice witch? I bet Reenie is the one who's been helping us!"

"I think you're right," said Sam.

They hurried to catch up with Mom and Dad. As they passed the white house, Sam nudged Becky with his elbow. "Look at that," he said nodding his head toward the house.

Becky followed his gaze to the porch of the white house and saw a very sleek black cat sitting on the top step washing up before dinner.

# Chapter 13

# MIRROR IMAGES
MIRROR IMAGES

"So, do you kids want to play a game or are you ready for bed?" Mom unlocked the door to Sam and Becky's room at the inn.

They had just returned from a wonderful dinner at the Harbor View Restaurant. Sam and Mom had tried the fresh lake trout while Dad had ordered sausages and **sauerkraut**. Becky had her favorite: spaghetti and meatballs.They topped everything off by sharing the biggest piece of chocolate pecan pie Sam and Becky had ever seen.

"I think I'm going to bed and read," said Becky.

"How about you, Sam?"

**SAUERKRAUT**
(SOW-er -krout)
Finely cut cabbage soaked in a mixture of salt and cabbage juice

101

"Oh, I think I'm going to reflect some on my day. Oooff…ouch Becky! Why did you do that?"

Becky sent him a warning look along with the jab in the stomach.

"Well," said Dad.

"That's an awfully deep subject, Dad," said Sam with a fake laugh.

"Very funny, son. Very funny. Very old, but very funny. As I started to say before I was so *rudely* interrupted by such a *poor* attempt at a joke, I think it's time for my nap."

"Good-night, Dad," said Becky. "Don't nap too long—you don't want to be late getting to bed."

"Honestly," said Mom, "You all are too much! I'm going to bed. Go brush your teeth and get ready for bed, my dears. I'll be back in just a few minutes to tuck you in. We don't have to check out of our rooms until 11:00, so let's plan to sleep in and we'll eat breakfast about 9:30."

"Sounds good to me," said Becky.

"Me too," agreed Sam.

"I already know what I'm going to have for breakfast," said Dad. "Thimbleberry pancakes. Mmm, mmm. I can't wait. Oh, and by the way, Sam, when *I* reflect on my day, I always use a mirror. Ha, ha, ha! Get it, a mirror? Ha, ha, ha! That's a good one. Did you get it, Alice? Yep, I'm still king of the jokers."

"I'm not sure that's a title I would want, dear," said Mom as she closed the door to Sam and Becky's room.

"Where's the riddle, Becky?"

"Right here in my pocket, why? You memorized everything it said."

"Dad's joke gave me an idea. You know how the letters look familiar, but we can't read them? Take a look at them when I hold them up in front of a mirror."

*"What?"*

"Take a look at the mirror."

Sam held the piece of paper up to the mirror in their bedroom. When Becky looked at the mirror, she saw a reflection of the writing.

"Mirror writing!" said Becky looking closer. "That's why it looks so familiar. It's like that old lady told Mom and Dad, 'There's a lot to see if you look at the right place.' If you look at the mirror, you can see the riddle. Read it, Sam. Read the riddle now."

"It still doesn't make much sense," said Sam. "'Ic who ur'? What does 'ick' mean? Or 'ur'? I don't understand."

Becky stared at the reflected image for a minute. "Try…try reading the letters one at a time. Read the words as words, but when you read the letters, just say the name of the letter."

Sam looked puzzled for a minute and then read, "I C who U R, I C what U C…oh, I get it now!

I see who you are,
I see what you see,
I know you,
Do you know me?

"That's it! That's the riddle!" Sam jumped up and down around the room. "This is great! I can't wait to tell Tom and Captain Pete that we know the riddle!"

"Wait a minute," he said, stopping in mid-leap. "We have the riddle, but we don't know the answer to the riddle."

"But don't you see," said Becky. "That's the answer too! The riddle is written in mirror writing and the answer to the riddle is a *mirror*!"

# Chapter 14
# REFLECT ON THIS

The next morning, Sam and Becky woke up early and dressed quickly. Becky left a note for Mom and Dad:

> Mom and Dad,
>
> Sam and I are visiting the fish museum one more time to see what we can see. We'll be back for breakfast by 9:30.
>
> Love,
> Becky

The museums and lighthouse didn't open to the public until 10:00, but since Captain

Pete had said he'd be there early, Sam and Becky decided to see if they could get in. They couldn't wait to tell Tom and the captain about the riddle.

The museum was unlocked, and when Sam and Becky went in, they saw Miss Maple typing at the computer at the front desk. She looked up hopefully, but her smile faded when she saw Sam and Becky. "You're looking for Captain Pete, aren't you?" she asked **wistfully**.

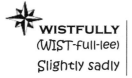

**WISTFULLY**
(WIST-full-lee)
Slightly sadly

"Well...uh...er...actually... we were looking for *you*, Miss Maple," said Sam with confidence. "We knew if anybody could tell us where the Captain was, it would...ah...it would be you."

Miss Maple chuckled as she pointed upstairs. "You're very smart, aren't you? I hope you can help Tom." Then she turned back to her computer.

Becky and Sam looked at each other in surprise. Then they raced up the stairs. "Captain Pete! Captain Pete! We have the riddle!" called Becky.

"And the answer," yelled Sam.

"Here now, what's all this shouting?" Captain Pete stood in front of the fireplace.

"Captain Pete, we figured out the riddle! And the answer," said Becky. "The clue is written in mirror writing. So when you put it in front of the mirror, you can read it, no problem. Look!"

Sam held the riddle in front of the cloud mirror where Captain Pete stood. "Look at the paper in the mirror, Captain Pete. See? You can read it, can't you?"

"Yes, I can! How did you…"

"And then once we read it," continued Sam, "Becky figured out the answer. The answer to the riddle is a mirror!"

As Sam said the words, a funny thing happened. Becky saw it first and her eyes got huge. "Sam! Captain Pete! Look!" she whispered.

As Becky, Sam, and Captain Pete stared at the mirror, a faint image began to appear. As it grew clearer, they saw the reflection of a tall boy standing behind them. The boy wore old-fashioned clothes and a great big smile.

"Is that you, Tom? We can see you! Look Sam, it's Tom!" cried Becky.

"I see, I see! Boy, can I ever see! Look at you, Tom. I mean, *look* at you! It's *really* good to see you!"

Tom was busy looking at his hands and feet. When he looked up again and saw himself in the mirror, he let out a whoop.

"I never thought I'd see myself again! I mean, I hoped I would, but I really didn't think it would happen! This is great! Hi, Captain Pete, sir," said Tom as he gave the captain a playful salute.

"Well, hello there, Tom Adams," replied the Captain, returning the salute. "May I say you're looking extremely well for a young man who's been under a curse for almost a hundred years. You look good, but how do you feel?"

"I feel great. And it's all because of you. How can I ever thank you enough? You're the best!"

"Don't forget Captain Pete," said Sam.

"Oh, the Captain and I go way back," said Tom. "I *hope* he knows how much I appreciate all he's done for me. I mean, he's the one who led me to you two and said you were the right ones to help me. He knows everything!"

"Don't know everything," said Captain Pete gruffly, "but I do know 'time's a'wastin'!"

"You're right," said Tom seriously. "I better get started on the next riddle. There are only three more days until the full moon."

"Do you even know where the next riddle is?" asked Sam.

"I don't know for sure. I've helped sailors all over the Great Lakes, but I thought I might go over to Bete Grise Bay because that's where it all started. That's where Malina put the curse on me.

"So…I should go now. Like the Captain said, I don't have much time left. Thanks again for all your help. I hope I see you again sometime—I know you'll see me!" And with a chuckle, Tom's new ghostly figure disappeared.

"Sam, we've got to go too. We promised Mom and Dad we'd be back for breakfast. Good-bye, Captain Pete. Thanks for everything. It was good to see you again."

"And good to see Tom, too," Sam added as he shook the captain's hand. "Good-bye, Captain."

Captain Pete watched Sam and Becky hurry down the stairs. Then he picked up his driftwood, sat down in the rocker, and started whittling. "So long to you all, but not good-bye. Not for long, anyway."

# Chapter 15
# WHAT'S NEXT?

Dad's thimbleberry pancakes were a big hit. The tiny berries gave the buckwheat pancakes a tangy sweetness. The waitress even brought over a sample of the inn's famous apple sausage to try with the pancakes.

"So what's next, Alice? Where are we going today?"

"Well, according to my schedule, we should drive up the peninsula and go over to the lighthouse at Marquette. I thought we could check out the…"

"Mom, have you thought about taking some time off and just exploring?" Becky's mind was racing. "You know, ignoring the schedule for a day or so, and driving over to...say..."

"...to Bete Grise Bay," Sam chimed in. "We could go over to Bete Grise Bay and...and...we could...we could...explore, like Becky said."

"Bete Grise Bay? What would we explore over there?"

"Well," said Sam, "there's...ah...there's the bay. Bete Grise Bay. And there's a shipwreck in the bay."

"Yes, Sam, but the shipwreck is underwater. And Bete Grise Bay is on the opposite side of the peninsula from here. I don't even know if there's a lighthouse there."

"Well then, maybe we should go find out if there is a lighthouse there," said Dad. "Sometimes it's fun to do something totally unplanned. Maybe we should just take the day and go explore with the kids. What do you think, Alice?"

"It's fine with me," agreed Mom, "I'd love a day just to play."

"Then it's all settled," said Dad, raising his glass of juice for a toast. "We're off on an unplanned adventure to Bete Grise Bay. Cheers!"

As Mom, Dad, Becky, and Sam clinked their glasses together, Becky said softly to Sam, "And here's to solving the third riddle."

Just at that moment, their waitress came over to the table. "My shift is up, so I'm leaving now. Did I hear you say you're going over to Bete Grise Bay? That's cool. There's a lot to see there if you find the right spot. 'Bye now, and good luck."

As the others continued talking about the unplanned day, Becky thought to herself, "Good luck? Why would she wish us good luck?"

Becky swiveled around in her chair and watched as the waitress prepared to leave. She put on her jacket and flipped her long, black

hair out from under the collar—but not before
Becky saw the embroidered outline of a smiling
black cat on the back of the jacket.

Becky poked Sam. "Sam! Our waitress—did
you see what color her eyes were?"

"No, why?"

"Look!"

As Becky and Sam watched, the waitress
with the long, black hair and the cat jacket
looked over at them and winked. Then she
put on her purple sunglasses and walked out
the door.

### THE END

# Just So You Know

Remember I said there were lots of great books to read and websites to visit? Well, here are some of my favorites.

## Books to Read

Berger, Todd R. and Daniel E. Dempster. *Lighthouses of the Great Lakes: Your Guide to the Region's Historic Lighthouses (Pictorial Discovery Guide)*. Stillwater, MN: Voyageur Press, Inc., 2002.

Clifford, Mary Louise and J. Candace Clifford. *Mind the Light, Katie: The History of Thirty-Three Female Lighthouse Keepers*. Alexandria, VA: Cypress Communications, 2006.

Grant, John and Ray Jones. *Legendary Lighthouses, Volume II: The Companion to the All New PBS Television Series*. Guilford, CT: The Globe Pequot Press, 2002.

## Websites to Visit

*Brockway Mountain Drive Web Tour*
www.cableamerica.com/Michigan/brock1.shtml

*The Keweenaw County Historical Society*
www.keweenawhistory.org/eh.html

*Exploring the North*
www.exploringthenorth.com/eagharbormi
www.exploringthenorth.com/bangor/bangor.html

*The* City of Bangor *and other shipwrecks*
www.ship-wreck.com/shipwreck/keweenaw/
bangor.html
www.pasty.com/pcam/ccmem
www.shipwreckmuseum.com *(thanks, Andrew)*